Mama's Leykach
(HONEY CAKE)

You'll need:

2 cups flour

1 tsp baking powder

3/4 tsp baking soda

1/8 tsp salt

2 eggs

1/2 cup sugar

1/2 cup honey

1/3 cup freshly brewed coffee

1-1/2 tbs salad oil

1 tsp vanilla extract

1 tsp lemon extract

Optional:

1/2 cup raisins, or

1/2 cup diced candied fruits, or

1/2 cup chopped almonds, walnuts, or filberts

Preheat oven to 325°. Make sure that an adult is with you when you are near the oven. Grease, flour, and set aside a loaf pan or two mini loaf pans. Sift together flour, baking powder, baking soda, and salt. Set aside dry ingredients. In another bowl, beat eggs. Add sugar and continue beating until mixture thickens. In a small bowl, mix together honey, brewed coffee, salad oil, vanilla and lemon extracts. Add this honey mixture to eggs and stir gently. Slowly add dry ingredients, about 1/2 cup at a time, and gently mix until all flour is blended with liquids. Pour into loaf pans and bake for 1 hour or until done. Test by poking a toothpick into center of cake. When toothpick comes out dry, the cake is finished baking.

ALADDIN
An imprint of Simon & Schuster Children's Publishing Division
1230 Avenue of the Americas New York, NY 10020
Text copyright © 1996 by Elsa Okon Rael. Illustrations copyright © 1996 by Marjorie Priceman
All rights reserved, including the right of reproduction in whole or in part in any form.
Book design by Paul Zakris. The text for this book was set in 14 point Stempel Schneidler.
The illustrations were rendered in gouache.
Manufactured in China
0318 SCP
10 9 8 7 6 5 4 3

The Library of Congress has cataloged the hardcover edition as follows:
Rael, Elsa Okon. What Zeesie saw on Delancey Street / by Elsa Okon Rael ;
illustrated by Marjorie Priceman.—1st ed.
p.   cm.
Summary: A young Jewish girl living on Manhattan's Lower East Side
attends her first "package party" where she learns about the traditions of
generosity, courage, and community among Jewish immigrants in the early 1900s.
ISBN 0-689-80549-7 (hc.)
1. Jews—New York (N. Y.)—Juvenile fiction. [1. Jews—New York (N. Y.)—
Fiction. 2. Emigration and immigration—Fiction.] I. Priceman, Marjorie,
ill. II. Title. PZ7.R1235Pac 1996 [E]—dc20 95-11321
ISBN 978-1-4169-7900-5 (proprietary)

061828.1K4/B1212/A7

WHAT Zeesie SAW ON Delancey STREET

BY Elsa Okon Rael ❧ ILLUSTRATED BY Marjorie Priceman

ALADDIN

New York London Toronto Sydney New Delhi

"Tonight, Mama? Really? I may go with you and Papa?"

Yes, this very night, on her seventh birthday, Zeesie was going to her first package party. Standing in front of the mirror, Zeesie climbed into her brand-new blue taffeta dress for the first time. She and Mama had gone all the way uptown to a BIG store, S. Klein On-the-Square on 14th Street, to buy it. And, if this weren't exciting enough, Bubbeh and Zaydeh had given Zeesie a dollar to celebrate her special day. A whole dollar bill—all for herself!

Zeesie carefully folded her birthday dollar into a little square and tucked it into the pocket of her new dress. She dreamed of how she would spend it. On the tin of twenty colored pencils? On the *Second Avenue Songbook*? Perhaps she could even buy something at the package party—just as all of the grown-ups would do!

Each family at the package party would bring a wrapped surprise package of homemade food to be sold at an auction. Earlier in the day, Zeesie had helped Mama bake her famous apple cake by sprinkling raisins onto the apple slices. And she had even helped Mama wrap the package filled with pickled herring, barley soup, flanken, pirogen, tsimmes, corn bread with charnishka seeds, and fresh pears— with brown paper and a ball of green twine.

Zeesie sang "Shain Vi Di L'Vone" as she braided her long auburn hair and smiled at her reflection. Oh, how very grown-up she felt!

It was still light when the family began the journey from Cannon Street to Delancey, and Zeesie skipped ahead of her parents. At Stanton Street, Mama paused at Mr. Singer's tailor shop window, where countless spools of thread, in every color imaginable, were piled high. "Let's *go*, Mama!" Zeesie tugged at Mama's sleeve.

At Rivington Street, where Zeesie usually stopped to visit the birds in the chicken yard, she did not even wave. "Not tonight!" she called out. Turning onto Delancey Street, Zeesie breezed by the fancy "Low-eez Delancey"—probably the biggest movie theater in the whole world—which charged ten cents admission. How many movies could she see for one dollar? she wondered with awe. "Delancey!" Zeesie cheered when she saw the street sign. "We're almost there, aren't we, Papa?

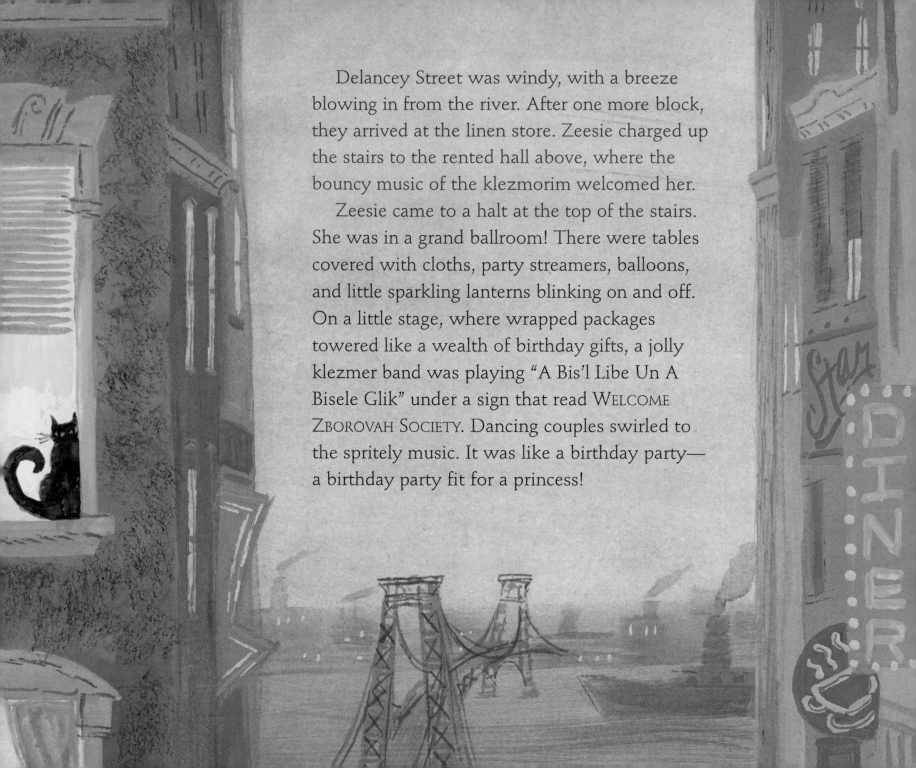

Delancey Street was windy, with a breeze blowing in from the river. After one more block, they arrived at the linen store. Zeesie charged up the stairs to the rented hall above, where the bouncy music of the klezmorim welcomed her.

Zeesie came to a halt at the top of the stairs. She was in a grand ballroom! There were tables covered with cloths, party streamers, balloons, and little sparkling lanterns blinking on and off. On a little stage, where wrapped packages towered like a wealth of birthday gifts, a jolly klezmer band was playing "A Bis'l Libe Un A Bisele Glik" under a sign that read WELCOME ZBOROVAH SOCIETY. Dancing couples swirled to the spritely music. It was like a birthday party—a birthday party fit for a princess!

Suddenly Zeesie was lifted high into the air and twirled about. Max Mendelson, Papa's best friend, always did that to her. "Not tonight!" she squealed. "I'm seven years old now, Max!"

Cousin Sheldon appeared from behind Max. Without even a hello, he grabbed Zeesie's arm and pulled her through the crowd. "Look at what *we* brought!" he boasted, flashing shiny new braces on his teeth and a hundred million freckles as he pointed to the largest package on the stage.

"Ours is bigger," Zeesie said proudly. "And you know what?" she whispered, pulling him closer. "I might even *buy* one of these packages tonight. I have a whole dollar bill!" She pulled it out, and Cousin Sheldon's eyes widened.

"Come now, Zeesie!" Zeesie heard Mama call out. "You're sitting over here with me, Papa, Uncle Yussie, and Tante Trina. The auction is about to begin!"

To great musical fanfare, Max Mendelson hopped onstage. "Welcome, lantsleit, members of the Zborovah Society," he said. "We gather once more for a good time and a time to do good. The money we raise tonight will help bring over more of our loved ones from Zborov to this wonderful America. So, be ready to open your hearts and your pockets and be generous."

Zeesie laughed as Max picked up the first package and pretended to stagger from its weight. "Ooh-ooh! That's got to be some kind of cement kugel in here," he bantered. "Do we have a lot of big spenders in the crowd? Good! Then let's start with, say . . . fifty cents?" Several voices shouted, "Fifty cents!"

"Do I hear seventy-five? Do I hear a dollar?"

Zeesie placed her hand on the folded dollar bill in her pocket.

"One dollar and *fifty* cents!" shouted a high bidder.

When Max held up a folded shopping bag, Papa bid high, hoping it was Mrs. Hercz's. With Papa's bid of two dollars and twenty-five cents, Max shouted, "Sold! To the father of the birthday girl, and the most beautiful little lady in the room!" Zeesie beamed as applause scattered across the hall.

Papa had guessed right—the package was Mrs. Hercz's, and it contained his favorite eggplant salad. For Mama, there were roasted chicken wings, and for Zeesie, a small bag of warm arbes, salted and peppered just the way she liked them.

Next, Uncle Yussie's bid bought a parcel beautifully wrapped in gift paper with pictures of lilacs. Zeesie looked at the pretty package longingly. "Would you like to open it, Zeesie?" Uncle Yussie invited.

Zeesie untied the bow, removed the paper, and lifted the lid of the shoe box slowly. "It's . . . it's . . . Uncle Yussie, it's a *brick*!" she gasped.

Uncle Yussie rubbed his chin. "So it is, Zeesie. I can't believe I paid two dollars for a brick!" The people at the next table laughed heartily.

"Why would anyone do such a mean thing?" Zeesie cried out indignantly.

"It's only a joke!" Papa reassured her. "There's plenty of food for everyone here." From all over the room, teasing friends and family began to bring food from their tables and pile it in front of Uncle Yussie. Soon there was more food before Uncle Yussie and Tante Trina than they could possibly eat. Zeesie laughed and slid an extra portion of warm arbes over to her own plate.

As they ate, Mr. Marcus, the candy store man, came to their table and tapped Papa on the shoulder. "It's your turn, Chaim," he said. Papa nodded and rose.

"Where are you going, Papa?" Zeesie asked.

"Into that room," he replied, pointing to a door.

"What's in there?"

Papa didn't answer. "I'll only be gone a minute," he reassured Zeesie.

"May I go with you?" she asked, not wanting to miss a thing.

"No. It's not permitted. I must go alone."

Zeesie watched Papa walk to the door. He knocked, waited a moment, and then entered, clicking the door shut behind him.

Zeesie's eyes never left the door. Why couldn't she go, too? She was old enough now to know about grown-up things!

When Papa came out and returned to the table, he tapped Uncle Yussie's shoulder. It was his turn now.

"Tell me what's behind the door," Zeesie begged. "Papa? Please?"

"Well, dear Zeesekeit," Papa began, "behind that door is a special room. We call it 'the money room.' Only men go in, one at a time. There, if a man has money to give, he leaves it. If he needs money, he takes it, but only as much as he needs. No one is supposed to know who has given or who has received. And, this is most important to know, it's as much a *mitzvah*— a good deed—to take when you need, as to give when you can."

"Did you give, Papa? Or did you take?"

Papa laughed. "That, my precious one, is a question never to be asked or answered. Never."

A money room? Maybe it was filled with treasure chests and gold coins and jewels and diamonds. Oh, why couldn't she see inside? Just one little look. A tiny peek. If only she could see—just once. What would happen, she wondered, if she dared to sneak in? If she were caught there? Would Mama angrily send her home to bed? Would Papa take away her birthday dollar? Her throat felt dry at the very thought—and yet—she was seven years old now!

Could she? Would she? Did she *dare*?

Zeesie rose from her chair. "I'm going to visit with Cousin Sheldon," she mumbled to whoever would hear. Everyone was chuckling at Uncle Yussie, who had just returned from the money room to find even more food at his table than when he'd left.

Zeesie gulped. She would have to slip by so many people to get over to the door with the tarnished brass knob. She plotted her path and cautiously threaded her way. At any moment, she expected to hear her name shouted out, calling her back to her seat.

Her heart thumped as she arrived at the door. The money room was empty, she knew, because she'd been watching it. Had anyone been watching her? She turned and scanned the room. No one had noticed where she had gone. She clenched the cold knob in her hand.

It must be now! Now! *Now!*

She turned the knob and slid into the room.

Where were the treasure chests filled with gold coins and jewels? Zeesie looked around at a damp, dark room with an unshaded lightbulb hanging over a small, rickety table. She saw stacks of old newspapers tied with rope near the far wall, and a broken chair in the corner, missing a seat. On the table, an old metal cash box with slots for coins and a section for bills barely gleamed under the harsh light.

Suddenly—*Tap-tap-tap!* Zeesie caught her breath. *Tap-tap-tap!*

Someone was at the door!

Zeesie dashed into the dark corner between the newspapers and the wall as the door opened. Her skin prickled as a man approached the table. Had she been seen? She looked to see, and—

Uh-oh, it was Max Mendelson! Zeesie hid her eyes. Papa had said no one should ever see such things, but it was too late.

Max hadn't seen her. Zeesie heard Max carefully count out eight dollar bills from the box and then recount them as he whispered a prayer in Hebrew. Max Mendelson. Jolly, funny, beloved old Max.

It's a mitzvah to take when you need, Papa had also said. Zeesie heard Max's need in his prayer, and it brought hot tears to her eyes, but she dared not breathe until he pocketed the money and left.

Zeesie knew she was where she should not have been and had seen what she should not have seen.

As Zeesie emerged from her hiding place, she took the dollar bill from her pocket, unfolded it, and placed it on top of the other bills. None of this could be told, she knew, remembering Papa's words. No one ever, ever, ever must know.

But she wasn't safe—not yet. She still had to make her way back to the table. Zeesie opened the door a crack and peeped out into the brightly lit room. No one was looking this way. No one had seen. But the next visitor to the money room would soon be on his way. Zeesie pressed her eyes shut and darted out into the party.

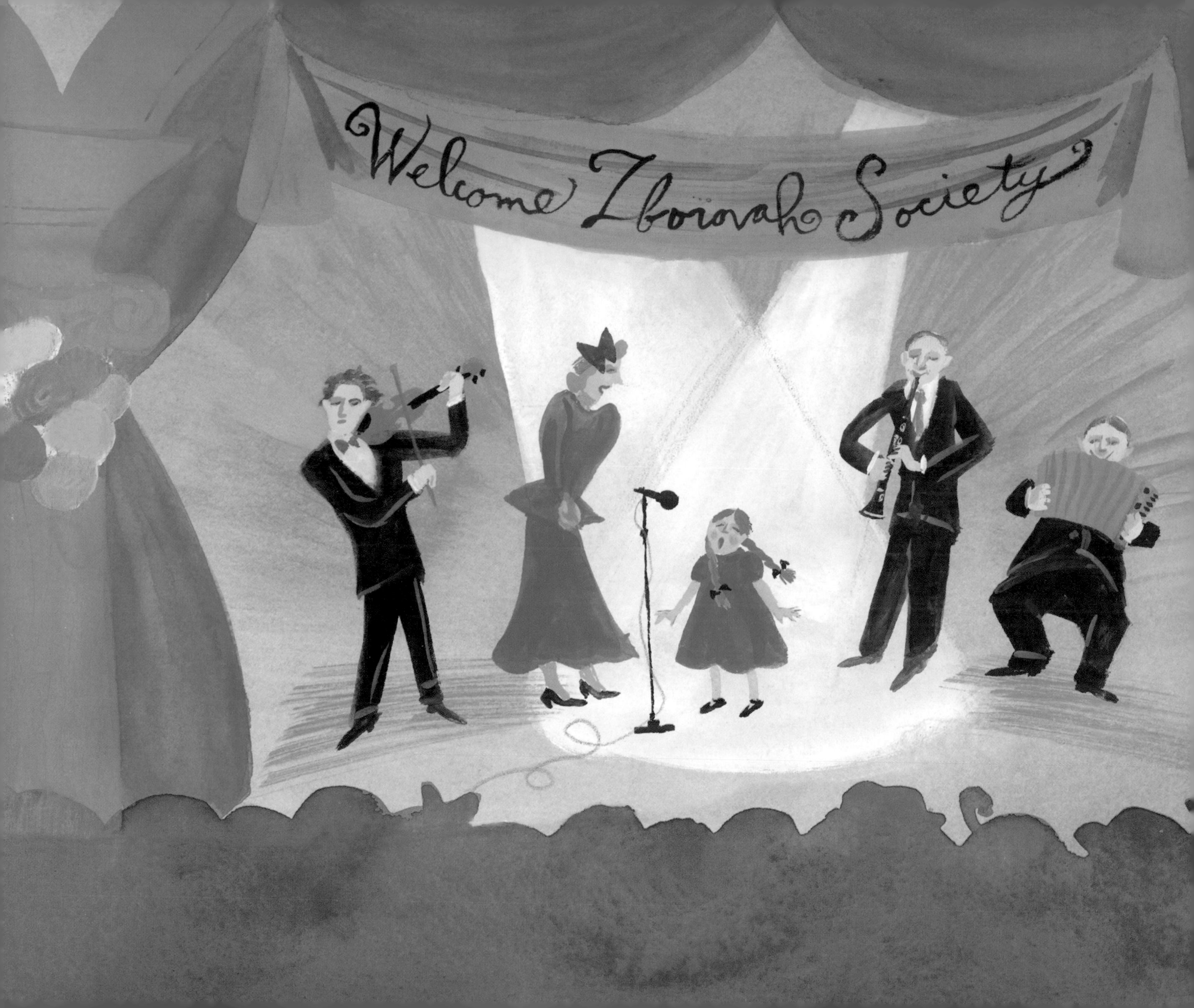
Welcome Zborovah Society

Halfway back to the table, Zeesie was just beginning to feel safe when Tante Trina's voice rang out sharply. "Zeesie! *There* you are!" Zeesie's knees grew weak. "Where were you? I was looking everywhere!" She grabbed Zeesie's hand and tugged her along to the stage. In a daze, Zeesie found herself trembling before a microphone. What was happening? Did everyone know what she had done? Oh, please, no!

"Don't be nervous, little darling. They're going to love you, I promise." Smiling, Tante Trina turned to the audience and announced, "My Zeeseleh-nieceleh makes her debut with me tonight as we sing 'Shain Vi Di L'Vone.' Maestro, if you please?"

They didn't know. No one knew. Zeesie heaved a deep sigh of relief and sang. She sang strongly, sweetly, surely. At the end, everyone stood, asking for more: *"Encore! Encore!"*

Afterward, Max Mendelson came to the stage and twirled Zeesie in the air, to the cheers of the crowd, and then carried her back to her family. "I see that the birthday girl is not only beautiful, but very brave, too. Right, Chaim?" he said to Papa.

At first, Zeesie was uncomfortable, remembering what she had seen in the money room. I'll never do anything like that again, she thought. But when she saw the amount of food on the table: knishes, a whole chicken, honey cake, gefilte fish, pickled beets, salads, soups, meatballs, mandelbrodt, kishka, sauerkraut, ruggelach, pickled watermelon rind, knockwurst—she burst out laughing.

Mama offered Zeesie the forgotten arbes. "Where were you, Zeesie?" she asked.

Zeesie smiled. "I was hunting for treasure, Mama."

"Well, I hope you found it," she said and added with a hug, "for I found mine in you. Happy birthday, Zeeseleh."

Her birthday. Yes. She thought about the day, the incredible day, as she ate the arbes, one by one. As for her birthday dollar, she knew it had been perfectly spent—and no one, no one would ever know if she had given or taken.

Author's Note

New York City's Lower East Side tenements were haven to thousands of immigrants and their families in the early years of the century. Memories of my own tenement childhood in the 1930s—the sounds of pushcarters hawking their wares; the smell of rain showers on hot summer concrete; the music of wayfaring singers and musicians in the backyard, to whom we tossed wrapped pennies; the taste of my Bubbeh's warm *challah* (braided egg bread) baked in a woodstove; the excitement of watching wedding vows being exchanged outdoors in the street (so that the Almighty might witness and partake in the festivities); playing stoopball, saloogie, ring-a-levio, immies, potsie, jacks; bathing in the kitchen washtub—all of these flash back with pungent clarity, as time smooths the brittle shoals of a lived life.

As for package parties, these fund-raisers were anticipated with particular relish by everyone. Most families had membership in *lantsleit* groups of families and friends who had emigrated from the same village abroad, organized around a common purpose. Burial societies, for example, purchased contiguous cemetery plots to maintain community even in the hereafter. Other groups, such as the one in this story, were organized to bring new immigrants to the Goldena Medina (America, the Golden Land).

For children, package parties meant music; laughter; scurrying in and around dancing parents; cousins, cousins, cousins, and the game of "cousin counting" (whoever had the most won); and spending time with the hardy pioneers who occasionally trekked to lower Manhattan from the far reaches of the Bronx.

—E. O. R.

GLOSSARY

"A Bis'l Libe Un A Bisele Glik" (ah BIS-el leeb oon ah BIS-eh-leh glick)—"A Little Love and a Bit of Luck," a Yiddish song made popular by Molly Picon and Jacob Rumshinsky in the 1920s

Arbes (AHR-bes)—chickpeas

Bubbeh and Zaydeh (BUB-beh, ZAY-deh)—grandmother and grandfather

Chaim (CHIY-yim)—a male first name, meaning "life"

Charnishka (CHAR-nish-ka)—large, black, spicy seeds used on the crust of rye corn bread, also called "black caraway"

Flanken (FLON-kin)—beef pot roast

Gefilte fish (geh-FIL-teh fish)—stuffed fish or ground fish rolled into spicy balls and gently simmered

Kishka (KISH-kah)—a sausage filled with flour, chicken fat, and onions

Klezmorim (klez-MOR-im)—a folk band consisting of a fiddle, clarinet, and accordion which, in this story, performed music from the Jewish theater

Knish (knish)—a large dumpling covered with flaky dough and filled with a choice of mashed potatoes, *kasha* (buckwheat groats), spinach, or meat

Knockwurst (NOK-versht)—spicy, garlic-flavored sausage

Kugel (KOO-gel)—baked pudding, usually made from potatoes or noodles

Lantsleit (LONT-zlite)—townspeople

Mandelbrodt (MON-del-broyt)—a semisweet bread-cake, usually with almonds

Pirogen (Pi-ROH-gen)—dumplings, usually filled with potatoes, cheese, or cheese and berries

Ruggelach (ROO-geh lach)—a butter pastry with nuts and cinnamon

Saurkraut (SOW-er-krowt)—salt-pickled cabbage

"Shain Vi Di L'Vone" (SHANE vee dee le-VOH-neh)—"Lovely as the Moonlight," a Yiddish song made popular by Chaim Tauber and Jacob Rumshinsky in the 1920s

Tante (TON-teh)—aunt

Tsimmes (TSIM-mess)—a mildly sweet compote usually made of carrots and prunes, often eaten with meat dishes

Zborov (ZBOR-uv)—a town in Poland

Zeesie, Zeesekeit (ZEE-see, ZEESE-kite)—Sweet One, Sweetness

Zeeseleh-Nieceleh (ZEE-seh-leh-NEE-seh-leh)—Sweet little niece

Zeesie's Tsimmes

There is a Yiddish expression sometimes used when someone creates a problem over a little thing. It may be said that he or she is making "a big *tsimmes*" out of nothing. Here is another kind of *tsimmes*—a recipe for a sweet relish often served with meat. Have an adult slice the fruits and vegetable for you, and make sure that the grown-up is with you when you are near the stove.

You'll need:
5 large carrots, sliced into circles
15 dried apricots, cut in half
15 pitted prunes, cut in quarters
1 cup raisins
3/4 cup honey or maple syrup

2 cups water
juice of 2 lemons
1 tbs vinegar
Zeesie's special ingredient:
2 tsp vanilla extract

Place all the ingredients into a saucepan and bring to a boil. Reduce heat to medium-low and simmer uncovered. Stir frequently. Cook for 45 minutes to 1 hour until carrots are soft. As the mixture cools, gently mash prunes and stir. Then add Zeesie's special ingredient and stir. *Tsimmes* is now ready to serve warm or, if you prefer, *tsimmes* is also delicious served cold.

Mama's Leykach
(HONEY CAKE)

You'll need:

2 cups flour

1 tsp baking powder

3/4 tsp baking soda

1/8 tsp salt

2 eggs

1/2 cup sugar

1/2 cup honey

1/3 cup freshly brewed coffee

1-1/2 tbs salad oil

1 tsp vanilla extract

1 tsp lemon extract

Optional:

1/2 cup raisins, or

1/2 cup diced candied fruits, or

1/2 cup chopped almonds, walnuts, or filberts

Preheat oven to 325°. Make sure that an adult is with you when you are near the oven. Grease, flour, and set aside a loaf pan or two mini loaf pans. Sift together flour, baking powder, baking soda, and salt. Set aside dry ingredients. In another bowl, beat eggs. Add sugar and continue beating until mixture thickens. In a small bowl, mix together honey, brewed coffee, salad oil, vanilla and lemon extracts. Add this honey mixture to eggs and stir gently. Slowly add dry ingredients, about 1/2 cup at a time, and gently mix until all flour is blended with liquids. Pour into loaf pans and bake for 1 hour or until done. Test by poking a toothpick into center of cake. When toothpick comes out dry, the cake is finished baking.